Archie The Spider: 4 Book Bundle

Kids Short Story Books

A Collection of four books
+ *1 Exclusive Bonus Story*

By
J W Paris

Illustrated by
Agnieszka Gorak

Contents

Table of Contents

Contents

Copyright

Published By

Deanburn Publications

Books in this series:
Book 1 Archie looks for a Friend
Book 2 Archie's Adventures Begin!
Book 3 Edinburgh Zoo Adventures
Book 4 Heroic Rescues & Water Monsters

Archie's Facebook Page:
www.facebook.com/ArchieTheSpider

Book 1: Archie Looks For A Friend

The Girl Next Door

"Why was I born a spider," Archie thought to himself. *"I could have been born a cuddly puppy, or even a cute kitten that everybody loved. I could be cuddled up in bed at night under a warm blanket with a hot water bottle maybe, just to keep out the cold. Instead though here I am, a poor hairy spider that nobody loves, stuck under a cold draughty floorboard.*

Surely someone out there would want to be my friend; that little girl next door is bound to like me if I just try very hard to get close and give her my biggest smile – yes that would do it I'm sure!"

Archie determined to get his coat on, and go out to see if he could find the little girl next door. He was a very lonely spider and all he really wanted was to find a friend. Poor Archie knows that some little girls and boys are scared of spiders, but he is determined to put this right and show them just how friendly spiders can be.

Out through the crack in the wall Archie ventured. He had to be very careful as birds in particular would think he was a healthy snack, and carry him away for lunch. Archie was a very clever spider though, and made his way carefully through the long grass to the house next door. It was difficult to climb up the steep steps to the house, and he had to spin a few webs to climb up, falling a few times in the process.

Finally however he made it to the top, and was relieved to see a crack under the door where he could manage to get into the house. It was getting dark outside now, so Archie was glad he had made it while he could still see clearly.

The little girl would be getting to bed just about now, so it was an ideal time for Archie to go and introduce himself.

"If I make it up the stairs in time for the bedtime story" Archie thought *"I could introduce myself to the girl and hear the story at the same time"*
This seemed like a great idea to Archie, so off he went top speed up the stairs to the little girl's bedroom. He knew the room was the last one on the right, as he had been there once before whilst getting out of the rain. The girl had been sleeping that time though, so he was not able to introduce himself. This time he must get there before she fell asleep.

The stair was easy to climb as it had a nice furry carpet, so he was able to run up the stair without having to spin any webs to help him. In no time at all he was at the top of the stairs and heading for the far away room.

Suddenly out of nowhere sprung the family dog! Rushing up to Archie it pressed its big wet nose against him, pinning poor Archie to the floor, and covering him with horrible snot so that he could hardly move as he was stuck to the floor!
"Oh help, what do I do now, that horrible dog is going to flatten me any minute; and just look at my good coat it's all soaking wet. I'll have to just make a run for it and try to get under the bedroom door as fast as I can" Thought Archie. He managed to free himself and took off full speed for the door, just in time he threw himself under the heavy door as the dog slammed against it, barking wildly at a jubilant Archie.
"Ha, he hasn't come up against a spider as smart as me before" thought Archie smugly as he looked up and saw the little girl all cosy in bed; waiting for her bedtime story. *"Now's my chance to go and introduce myself to my new friend"* With that he slowly climbed up the blanket trailing over the bed.
It was a tough climb for Archie, as the bed was as high as a mountain to him. However he did manage to scramble up over the top, and was just gathering his breath to say hello when suddenly .. *"Shreeekkkk"* the little girl screamed out at the top of her voice, and again *"shreeekkk help mummy…"*

Just then the door burst open and the little girl's mummy came charging into the room. She immediately set her eyes on Archie, who had just made it up on to the pillow to say hello to his new friend. She lunged towards him with a rolled up newspaper, and **whacked** the pillow just missing Archie, but knocking him flying through the air as the pillow bounced up with the impact of the newspaper.

Poor Archie found himself on the floor, running for the open door to make his escape. He was sure he would make it; until the dog came barging in. Immediately it set it's beady eyes upon Archie, who was quite winded by this time and could hardly catch his breath.
The dog lunged at him and managed to grab him by one of his legs.
"Ouch, help" cried Archie.
However no-one would listen to him shouting for help as the dog ran off out of the room and down the stairs, with a very sore Archie dangling from it's mouth.
Still luck was with him, for as the dog hit the rug at the bottom of the stairs, it slid across the floor carrying the dog with it. The dog slammed against the wall, releasing its grip on Archie for just a moment. It was all Archie needed. Dropping quickly to the floor Archie sped to the skirting and slid under a tiny gap, just as the big sharp teeth of the dog snapped shut – on fresh air.

Archie had escaped disaster. Through the gap he went, and managed to find his way to the outside. Panting heavily with all the exertion and a bit frightened by his narrow escape; Archie headed home to bandage his leg and have a drink of water. *"I almost made it that time"* he said to himself *"If only that little girl had given me a chance, I'm sure we could have been good friends"*

Archie was not too discouraged though, and he would try again as he was a lonely spider desperate for company. Already he was thinking about his next plan to find a new friend.

**

A Surprise Encounter

It was another day, and Archie was feeling very sorry for himself. His little leg was hurting and he was all bruised with his encounter with that horrible dog. Worse than that was his mum insisting that he could not go out again, until he was all better.

"Never mind" Thought Archie *"I know for a fact that the little girl has a brother, and everyone knows that boys are braver than girls!"*

Archie still had a lot to learn about boys and girls, *"So tomorrow when mum lets me out, I'll sneak into the house again and see if I can get close to the little boy – he's bound to like me, and want to be my friend"*

The next day Archie pleaded with his mother to let him go out to play in the garden *"Ok then"* His mother *said* *"But just be sure you do not get into trouble again, and stay away from birds and horrible dogs !"*

Archie ran off to find his jacket, as it was very cold outside and he did not want to freeze before he got across the lawn to the next door house. Here is where he would be successful, he thought to himself; and at last make a friend that he could talk to and play games with.

Poor Archie still though that if only he had a chance to meet them, then these children would love to be his friend. With that comforting thought

Archie headed for the crack in the wall, and went outside.
He did not know it, but great danger was waiting for him..

Sitting on the branch of a tall tree, a large yellow beady eye looked down upon Archie.
"A juicy fat spider" The Blackbird thought *"just what I need for breakfast!"*
Swooping down from the tree the bird headed straight for Archie just making his way across the lawn. Archie was daydreaming to himself, and so was not aware of the great danger he was in.
"I can't wait to get to see that little boy, he's sure to be a lot braver and at least let me close enough to speak to him"
"Arrgghhh!" Archie screamed as almost too late, he spotted a shadow descending over him. The big yellow beak of the blackbird opened wide to swallow up Archie, who was just passing an empty bottle lying on the grass at that very moment. He dived into the neck of the bottle, just as the blackbird was about to swallow him whole.

Peck Peck Peck,
The blackbird pecked away furiously at the glass bottle. It could see Archie hiding inside, but it could not break the strong glass.
"Phew, that was a close one" thought Archie, as he tried to catch his breath. Then suddenly a realization came to him; this was the same bird

that had attacked him when he was only a baby, and resulted in him being blind in one of his 4 eyes! He'd had to wear an eye patch since that time. The truth was though that this did not bother him too much at all, because he looked like a pirate-which he thought was rather cool; and besides, he still had another three eyes to see with! Archie sat down on the glass bottom, as he was feeling quite unwell at the thought.

"It's no use at all feeling sorry for myself, I'll really have to find a way out of here or I am in real trouble, especially if the bird manages to break this bottle".

As Archie was thinking this, he began to feel very warm. To start with he thought that he was just frightened and that was why he was getting hot and bothered, so he took off his little jacket to cool down. Then he noticed that the sun, which had been low in the sky up till now, had begun to get higher in the sky and was now shining on the glass bottle. The temperature was rising fast, and Archie started to panic!

Looking out through the glass, Archie could see that the blackbird had moved away, but was now sitting on a branch just a few feet away looking greedily down on Archie and thinking of its spider breakfast. He peeked outside and saw that he was not far from the hedge at the side of the garden.

"I wonder if I could just jump out quickly and make a run for that hedge, surely that fat bird cannot be faster than me"

Archie still had a lot to learn about how fast birds were as well.

He slowly sneaked up to the opening at the neck of the bottle, and seeing the coast was clear, put one foot out of the opening…**BANG!!** The big yellow beak slammed against the glass, just missing Archie's foot and sending him tumbling back inside the bottle! He rolled along the bottom coming to rest against the side; where the horrible bird again set to work trying to get to him through the glass.

Peck Peck Peck, on and on it went, determined to make breakfast out of poor Archie; who now knew just how fast birds can be!

"What do I do now? That creature is not going to let me out, and I'm beginning to feel very dizzy with this heat"

The temperature was rising fast, and unless Archie could find a way out of this bottle without getting eaten then he would surely perish in the heat.

He was just beginning to despair when a movement outside caught his eye – well his three eyes to be exact! A slight movement in the bushes behind the blackbird, then **WHAM!** His whole world turned upside down. The bottle rolled and rolled, spinning Archie round about and upside down, till suddenly it came to a halt underneath the bushes. Archie got himself together and without hesitation, he grabbed his jacket and launched himself out of the bottle, disappearing under a large stone.

After a few moments he peaked out from under the rock, to see just what had happened. Right there where the bottle had been, stood a fluffy kitten. It was a white kitten with a black patch of hair over one of its eyes, which were bright emerald green and very mischievous looking to Archie!; and was standing with a feather hanging from its mouth!

"Ha ha" Archie whooped, *"the kitten has chased away the bird and I'm free again!"*
He was jubilant, and racing out from under the rock, jumped up and down with joy. The blackbird meanwhile was up on the tree branch minus a tail feather, promising himself that this was not the last of the matter, and the next time that fat spider came out; he would have him!
Just as he was celebrating his good fortune, a dark shadow was cast over him, Archie froze where he was. The shadow grew bigger and bigger, until all of a sudden Archie felt a hot breath down the back of his neck.
"Oh how stupid am I" he thought to himself. *"I've been so busy celebrating my good fortune that I have not noticed the kitten creeping up on me, and now I'm going to be eaten!"*
He closed his eyes tightly and waited, as he was well exposed and had nowhere to run to.

Suddenly he was aware of a noise like a motor car engine. A rumbling purring noise, was all around him. He felt a cold wet thing brushing up against him, and was forced to open his eyes. He was facing a cold wet nose, that had covered him in wet snot!

Not quite understanding just what was going on, he looked up at the kitten. Looking down on Archie the kitten smiled and rubbed his face against the spider. Then suddenly without any warning, it bounded away to play with a ball of cotton grass.

Archie was confused, but not wasting any time, he rushed away towards home. Getting to the crack in the wall he quickly climbed up his spider-web ladder and rushed inside to safety.

"I really do not understand what went on there." Archie thought to himself. *"Could it be that the kitten is lonely like me perhaps?"* Then he remembered something about the cat. *"It had a patch of black fur over one of its eyes as well. Maybe I've found a pirate cat!"*

With that thought in his head, Archie went for a little sleep. It had been a busy morning, and he was quite exhausted after all the drama. His little bandaged leg was throbbing a little, but not too bad considering all the excitement. Tomorrow would be another day of adventure he was sure of it. However if Archie really knew what tomorrow would bring – he would never get to sleep!

**

Archie Finds A Friend

It was another day, and Archie was desperate to get outside and see if he could try again to get to the house next door and speak to the little boy. He was sure that he could talk him around to being his friend, if he could just put on his friendliest smile and show the boy that he was not a scary, hairy spider! Archie had got a bit of a scolding when he told his mum what had happened the previous day, but he had managed to convince her that today would be different, and he would not get into trouble again.

His sore leg was a lot better today, so he felt happy as he slid down his web ladder and out into the sunshine; all the while looking out for any great big blackbirds with their bright yellow beaks just waiting to gobble him up!
When he was sure the coast was clear he set of cautiously across the garden.
"What is that terrible noise coming from across the garden" He thought to himself. **"Sounds like that horrible dog from next door is bullying someone again"**
He headed off for the direction of the noise, thinking to himself that if the dog was out, he might as well know where it was so that he could stay out of the way.

As he drew nearer, so the noise got louder, yet he could not see anything because the noise was coming from behind a big old shed that was blocking his view.

"Bark bark bark bark"

It sounded like the dog was making a real fuss. As he cautiously approached the shed, moving very slowly so as not to let anyone know he was coming; he finally reached it. He slowly peeked around the corner of the shed; there was the horrible dog that almost had him eaten, when he caught Archie in the house! It was jumping up and down on four legs and trying to get to something that was up the tree. Archie leaned forward just a little closer to see what it was after…there was the white kitten that had rescued him yesterday!

"Meeoowww" the kitten cried from the flimsy tree branch. *"Won't somebody save me from this horrible dog?"* Archie gave a gasp as he could see the branch that the kitten was on was far too thin and it looked about to break – dropping the poor kitten straight into the dogs open jaws!

"What can I do," panicked Archie *" I'm just a little spider, and that is a great big dog out there. If I go anywhere near it I'll be eaten up and that will be the end of poor Archie!"*

He wracked his tiny brains for an idea to help save the kitten, which was now in real trouble as the thin branch threatened to break at any moment.

Suddenly he had an idea *"I know; I'll climb up this old shed and let the kitten that I am here. Maybe it will be encouraged to hold on a bit longer while I get a plan together!"*
With that, he scrambled up the side of the shed in no time – he was a spider after all and climbing was his specialty.

He reached the top of the shed, which was just a short distance from the tree, but too far for the cat to reach with a single jump, Archie realized. He decided to try shouting to the kitten to let her know that he was there.
"Hey, Hey kitten." The kitten looked across to the sound of Archie's tiny voice, and caught sight of him on the top of the shed. She looked terrified and was hanging on for dear life.
"What's your name," Archie called out to the kitten.
"Help, help. My name is Suzie, and this horrible dog is about to eat me up if I fall from this branch. I can't hold on much longer!"
"Don't worry and try to hang on a bit longer, I think I have an idea that will help you."
Archie had thought of a cunning plan – he was a very clever spider after all, much too clever for that stupid dog he thought to himself.
"Listen closely, I've got an idea," Archie shouted across to Suzie. *" I'm going to run to the far away end of the roof and then I'm going to distract that horrible dog so that he will chase me. When he*

comes running after me, then you can make your escape and jump up here with me." "Please hurry, cried Suzie I'm slipping and can't hold on much longer!"

Archie quickly scrambled to the far end of the roof away from the dog. He was sure this would work, but he had to hurry or poor Suzie would be eaten! When he reached the far end, he quickly spun a web and dropped down of the roof to within just inches from the ground.

 "Hey Ugly!" Archie screamed at the dog. *"You have a nose like a squashed tomato!"*
The dog however was making so much nose that he could not even hear Archie's insults.
"Bark, bark, bark, bark" it went on and on.
Jumping around the bottom of the tree, it could see that the kitten was slipping and he was sure that soon he would have it for breakfast!

Archie was a bit lost as to what to do next. *"Maybe this was not such a good idea after all, if he can't hear me then how can I get him distracted"*
Suddenly there was a pause in the barking as the dog stopped for breath. Archie took his chance and at the very top of his lungs cried out
"Hey smelly, why don't you pick on some-one your own size!"
Archie was of course tiny compared to the dog, but he was feeling very brave; and showing off a bit in front of Suzie!

It worked! The dog looked over towards the sound of the tiny voice, and his dark beady eyes immediately locked onto Archie. Recognizing Archie as the spider that he lost in the house, and got a sore head as a result of banging into the wall; he rushed straight towards Archie.

Hanging just above the ground Archie had to move very fast, as the dog was almost upon him in no time. Zoom, Archie sped up the line that he had spun at a record speed. Just out of the dogs reach, he stopped and started yelling insults at the dog, who's attention was now fully focused on Archie! Suzie did not hesitate, for just at that moment she was losing her grip and was about to fall. Seeing the dog running toward Archie, she immediately dropped to the ground and rushed towards the shed. The dog turned at the sound, and immediately ran back towards the kitten. He lunged towards Suzie with his big jaws open to eat her up; too late! Suzie managed to leap up the side of the shed, as only cats can do when they are very scared.

"Hey Hey, you saved me!"

Suzie was leaping up and down for joy on the top of the shed roof. She was so happy in fact that Archie thought he was going to be stomped on, and had to jump around himself to avoid it! He was delighted with the way it had all worked out to plan, and had a big grin all over his face. Suzie rolled on the roof purring and meowing, she had a very close escape and she knew it.

"That was a great plan, I owe you my life as that horrible dog would certainly eaten me if I had fallen off the tree. You are an incredibly brave little spider!
"My name is Archie" he said.
"Well Archie, I am very pleased to know your name. I did mean to talk to you the other day when you were trapped in the bottle, but I got distracted with that cotton ball – I'm very easily distracted you see!"

They were both jubilant and the dog of course was not happy! The problem they now had of course was that the dog was just waiting for them to come down from the shed roof – where he could pounce upon them! Archie and Suzie were not worried though; they would simply lie down on the flat roof of the shed until the dog got bored. Meanwhile they had a lot to talk about, and stories to share.
It took a long time for the dog to get bored, much longer than they thought. Eventually though he went back to his own garden, sneaking under a gap in the fence. It was quite late though and Archie knew that his mum would be getting worried. He looked across the garden and realized that he had travelled much further than he thought, and it would take him a while to get home. Worse than that, he spotted his old enemy the blackbird high up on a tree, staring down with hungry eyes!
Archie was afraid.

He pointed out his problem to Suzie, and she just laughed! *"This is very serious"* Archie cried, *"why are you laughing?"*

Suzie looked at him with a twinkle in her eye. *"I'm laughing because I know how you can get home in just a few seconds!"*

Archie looked at her as if she were quite mad. *"Jump on my back, and we can be across the garden before you know it. That big bird daren't touch you while I'm around!"*

Archie grinned a big grin, *"you would do that for me?"* *"Of course, you saved my life didn't you? The least I can do is get you home safe and sound!"*

"Does this mean we are friends?" Archie asked. *"Of course we're friends, your my best friend in the whole world now!"*

Archie was delighted, he'd rescued a kitten and found a friend all at the same time.

He jumped on Suzie's back, and she jumped gracefully down from the shed. Archie held on tight as she bounded across the lawn, towards his web-ladder. In a few seconds, just as she had said, they were safely at Archie's home. *"Will you manage to get home by yourself ok"* He said to Suzie,

"That's no problem, I stay with my mistress just a couple of houses away. Would you like to meet up again sometime?" She looked hopefully towards Archie.

"That would be just GREAT," he said.

They both said their farewells, and headed home. Archie scooted up his web-ladder, while Suzie bounded across to her house. *"I can't wait to tell mum, I've found a great friend and now can have some company when I go out to play."*
He headed into the house, dreaming about all the adventures he would have with his new friend Suzie.

**

Book 2: Archie's Adventures Begin!

Archie Gets Attacked!

Archie gave a big yawn as he woke up from a deep sleep. His mummy was shouting him down for breakfast, but he was nice and cosy in his web-bed and did not really want to get up. He closed his eyes again for just a moment,
 "just a few more minutes and I will get out of this cosy bed." Archie thought to himself. His mother however had other plans, and promptly picked him up and carried him down to breakfast. Poor Archie was half sleeping and a bit dozy, however he soon woke up and had his breakfast of dried fly porridge and some milk.

The day had only just begun, and Archie was suddenly very keen to go outside to play with his new friend Suzie the kitten.

"I wonder if I will see her today" Archie thought. He remembered the fun they had had the previous day, when he had managed to rescue Suzie from the horrible neighbor's dog from next door.

When he told his mother about all the excitement, she was very afraid for Archie. However he had managed to persuaded his mum that the kitten was a good friend, and that he would bring her round to see her just as soon as he could. This helped a lot, and Archie's mother said that she would be happy to meet his new friend the next time she came by. Archie put on his little jacket and shoes and headed outside. It was a beautiful sunny morning as he poked his head out to see if all was clear, but there was no sign of Suzie.

"Never mind, she is probably still fast asleep in bed." He thought to himself. *"I know, I'll head over to that high fence and climb to the top and see if I can see her garden from there, and if she is outside I can maybe shout over to her!"*
So off Archie went, to get to the other side of the garden so that he could climb the fence. He was only a small spider with little legs, so it took some time to get to the other side, in fact he was wishing he had taken a drink of water with him as the sun was rising and it was getting a bit warm.

"Never mind, I'll soon be in the shade of that nice bush, and get myself cooled down a little."
Thought Archie.
All the time Archie was travelling across the open lawn however, he did not think of looking up, as he was too busy thinking of his friend Suzie. The blackbird peered down at the movement in the grass.

"Ah Ha, I do believe that creature is the very same spider that escaped from me just yesterday; and almost got me eaten by that kitten! Now I will have my revenge – and my breakfast at the same time!"

The blackbird swooped down towards Archie. Too late, poor Archie seen the shadow over him and tried to run for cover.

"I HAVE YOU NOW!" the blackbird triumphantly screeched, as it pinned Archie to the ground with a big knobbly foot. *"You're not so clever now are you little spider?"* the bird mockingly said to Archie *"Where is your friend now eh? I'm going to eat you all up, and enjoy every morsel – even your spindly little legs!"*

The blackbird opened his beak wide to swallow up Archie. *"Stop, wait just a minute please"* Archie pleaded. He was in real trouble this time, and had to do some fast thinking.

"Ok, spider," said the blackbird *"what have you got to say before I gobble you up."*

Archie though quickly *"I would just like to know your name, before you eat me. You are obviously a very clever bird to catch me like this; you must be the smartest bird in the whole district!"*

At this, the blackbird stopped and preened himself. He was a very proud bird, and did indeed think that he was exceptionally clever.

"Well I must say that I cannot disagree with you spider, there is no-one smarter than me in the entire bird kingdom!"

Archie suddenly realised that he could maybe get out of this predicament.

"then please Mr blackbird, could I know your name before you eat me?"

"Well I suppose it cannot do any harm spider, my name is Jet"

"Well my name is Archie." Said the spider quickly. *"Please can I ask you Jet, why do you want to eat me, I could be your friend and help you out with things."*

"Ha ha ha, you have to be kidding me" said the blackbird *"what could you possibly do for me?"* All the time they were talking, a small furry kitten was sneaking its way across the grass. Suzie had seen the predicament that Archie was in and was trying to get to him before the blackbird gobbled him up.

"Oh no, I'm going to be too late" Suzie thought to herself *"that horrible blackbird is going to eat him before I can get there."*

However Archie had spotted Suzie as she was coming up behind the blackbird, and had thought of a clever plan.

"Do you remember the kitten that rescued me yesterday?" Archie asked the bird.

Jet glared down at the spider, with its beady eye.

"Are you trying to annoy me, it almost bit my tail off!" The blackbird said, getting ready to gobble Archie up and get it over with.

"No no, not at all Mr blackbird, its just that she is a good friend of mine; and I could ask her to be your friend also if you liked?"

Suzie meanwhile was getting closer to her friend Archie, almost close enough to pounce on the blackbird, with its big yellow beak and piercing eyes.

"To be my friend eh?" Jet stopped and thought about it *"what would be in it for me?"* said the blackbird.

Archie blurted out *"Well I know you are very clever and could easily fool a little kitten, but wouldn't it be nice if you did not always have to look over your shoulder all the time in case she is there? In fact if she were your friend, then she could look out for you and chase away your enemies as well."*

The blackbird looked down on this little spider *"He really is almost as smart as me."* The blackbird thought.

Suzie meanwhile had gotten quite close, and crouched down ready to pounce on the blackbird and save Archie if she could.

"Ok spider, what you say is quite interesting." *"please call me Archie"* he said.

"Ok Archie, I think I might be interested, if your friend will agree. We could all shake hands and form a real friendship, so that none of us had to be afraid in our own garden – does that sound good to you?"

Archie looked past the blackbird just as Suzie was about to launch herself onto the bird. *"STOP"* Archie shouted at the top of his voice.

"Whaaaatt the.." The blackbird quickly looked around and spotted Suzie mid-flight, and just in time flew up to an overhanging branch. Suzie

landed just inches away from Archie, almost flattening him as she did so.

"Oh Archie, are you all right?"

"I'm great Suzie, thank you for coming to rescue me – but you almost killed our new friend!" Archie looked at Suzie with a huge grin on his face.

"New friend, what do you mean Archie?" Archie explained everything to Suzie as Jet the blackbird looked down on them with his yellow eye.

"I don't know if I trust that bird, Archie." said Suzie, *"He almost had you eaten a few moments ago!"*

"But I never hurt him at all," the blackbird called down, *"in fact I do think that we could all be friends. Let's just call it a terrible misunderstanding, after all it is a big garden and we could all share it no problem. It might be good to have a friend – I think that Archie is right."* The blackbird was well aware that he had had a close call, and that Archie had probably saved his life by calling out for the kitten to stop. It did not take him long to decide that it would be better to make friends, than to be enemies of this pair of adventurers.

"Ok blackbird, come down and we can shake hands over it" said Suzie as Archie nodded his head enthusiastically.

"Ha, if I fly down, what's to stop you eating me?" Said Jet *"nothing at all"* Suzie said with a smile. *"But Archie is my best friend and if he*

says that it is all right, then I will agree to it. You can come and join us if you like; if not then go away – I don't care really."
Jet thought for a moment; then decided to take a risk and fly down to them.

"Well done Jet," said Archie as he lifted his little arm to shake hands *"come on Suzie, shake hands with Jet"* Archie looked on as they shook hands, it was a huge moment. Out of a very dangerous situation had come a great opportunity, and now he had two new friends.

Life was now just full of opportunities and he could see great adventures ahead for the three of them. They all made a promise to stick together, then Archie jumped on Suzie's back and bounded away across the garden. *"Did I really just make friends with a spider and a kitten?"* thought Jet who was a bit confused by the turn of events. *"It is indeed a strange world sometimes; still it can't harm to have a couple of extra friends to help me if I need it."*
The blackbird flew off to his nest to think about the mornings events. Tomorrow would be another day – and who knew just what wonders it would bring.

**

Archie's Mum Meets His New Friends

Archie's mum Agnes, was not really looking forward to meeting his new friend Suzie. For the simple reason that Suzie was a kitten, and they were known to play with spiders – often harming them in the process!

However Archie was really excited to bring Suzie home to show her, so she allowed him to make the arrangements. She would make a little dinner of real Scottish oatcakes and milk for them to share, and just prayed that it would be ok.

Archie was a lonely little boy, as all of his older siblings had moved away from home, and father had disappeared to who-knows-where; she knew that he really needed some friends to call his own that would keep him company. Perhaps even offer him some protection in this often scary world, *"who knows"* she thought "perhaps his new friends – even that blackbird – would be a great blessing for them all" She put on her apron and set to work preparing the food for them.

Archie meanwhile was 'beside himself' with excitement. Suzie was coming to meet his mum and they were all to have snacks together! He really hoped that his mum would like Suzie, as she really was a good friend that had rescued him twice already, if he hadn't have known her, then that blackbird would surely have eaten him for breakfast when he had the chance.

"All is fine now though," he thought to himself *"even that nasty blackbird – responsible for my one blind eye - could change and be a friend rather than an enemy. You just never know how things are going to turn out sometimes."* With these thoughts he went out to welcome Suzie, who was herself a bit nervous about meeting Archie's mum. *"I've never met a spider's mum before,"* Suzie was thinking to herself *"I wonder if I call her 'Ma' or Mrs Brown, or maybe just Agnes. It's all new to me, I'll just be polite and see how things go"*

Suzie seen Archie coming out to meet her, so she raced across the garden and jumped over his head playfully. *"Hi Archie,"* she called out *"bet you can't catch me! Ha ha"* *"Oh, you don't think so eh."* Archie called out, then he whipped up a quick lasso made from spun silk and neatly threw it over Suzie's head as she ran past.

"Hey hey, I've got you" he cried out, and quickly clambered up the silk rope and jumped onto Suzie's back. Suzie meanwhile took off across the garden again while Archie held on with all eight legs, bumping up and down on the kittens back. *"This is fantastic Suzie"* he called out to her, *"go faster!"*

"You had better not fall off then, or your mother will kill me" she laughed at Archie as he held on to the lasso. *"Don't worry about me – this is GREAT!"*

After a couple of times around the garden, the kitten slowed up in front of Archie's house panting slightly for breath. Archie too was exhausted with excitement and with holding on to Suzie as she went wild about the garden.

Archie's mother appeared at the door, and immediately stepped back slightly when she saw Suzie the kitten.

"Well, she may be just a kitten," Agnes thought *"but she surely is very big and hairy! I do hope Archie knows what he is doing."*

"Hey mum" Archie called out *"This is my best friend Suzie, come out and meet her!"*

Agnes carefully stepped out of the house and walked across to meet Suzie. She was still slightly scared of this kitten, and so was a little reluctant to go right up to her. Archie however was perfectly at ease and jumped down from Suzie's back to make the introductions.

"Mummy, this is Suzie my best friend, and Suzie, this is my mother Mrs Brown"

Suzie crouched down to get closer and said in her most polite voice *"Good morning Mrs Brown, it is a real pleasure to meet you."*

"Oh please just call be Agnes, and it is a real pleasure to meet you also, even if you do seem a little large and scary to a small spider like me!"

They all laughed together, and Agnes got them sat down to eat the cookies and milk picnic she had prepared for them. It was a lovely afternoon with some nice warm sunshine, and the birds singing in the trees. In fact one bird – the blackbird Jet, was singing particularly loud, as he had seen the little picnic from high up in his tree; and really wanted to join his new friends who seemed to be having a such great time eating and laughing.

He went up to the highest branch and sung just as loud as he could, hoping to catch their attention. Agnes was the first to notice *"listen to that beautiful bird-song Archie, it's coming from that bird way high up in the tree"* Archie and Suzie both looked up to where she was pointing.

"Hey that's Jet !" Archie exclaimed.

"JET…..JET.." Archie called out at the top of his little lungs. Jet looked down at them.

"Why not join us for cookies and milk, and you can meet my mother as well." Archie shouted up to Jet.

Immediately Jet the blackbird swooped down to join them, with a big flapping of wings and a rush of air, he landed right next to Suzie – who was still a little suspicious of the blackbird.

Agnes meanwhile had vanished behind a rock, as she saw this blackbird with its bright yellow beak and piercing eyes descend towards them.

Archie called out to her *"Mum, it's ok, Jet is our friend now – isn't that right Jet?"*

Jet nodded his head vigorously, *"Certainly is, and I'm really pleased to be invited to your picnic!"* He said hungrily eyeing up the cookies and the Scottish oatcakes. Archie's mum came out from behind the rock, and Archie made the introductions again.

"I must be honest Jet, you gave me a big fright dropping down on us like that – I'm really glad that you are Archie's friend. You as well Suzie; I couldn't ask for better companions for my little boy and do hope that you will take care of him when he's out playing." "MUM.. your embarrassing me in front of my friends now!"* Archie said indignantly. They all laughed playfully at Archie's red face, and got stuck in to their picnic.

After the food was finished they all lay back in the sun, enjoying each other's company and getting drowsy from the heat and a full tummy. Archie climbed up on Suzie's belly, as she lay half sleeping on her side.

Suddenly though, he was aware that she was making a terrible noise from her chest, that seemed to rumble right through the little spider. *"Oh Suzie, what's wrong?"* Archie said, getting a little alarmed that his friend was not well. *"Wrong? Why there's nothing wrong with me"* Suzie said sleepily, just a little puzzled at the question. *"But I hear a great noise coming from your chest Suzie – I think you are not well maybe!"* Suzie laughed as she realised what Archie was talking about. *"Ha ha, that's just what happens when I am happy! I make this purring sound from my chest – I can't help it really, it just means that I am contented and pleased to be with you!"*

Archie looked at Suzie in wonder, then looked across at his mum who was nodding and smiling at the same time. Archie sighed a sigh of relief, and settled down into Suzie's fur, listening to the rhythmic purring sound from Suzie and being lulled into sleep by the rising and falling of her chest.

Jet meanwhile decided that he was not going to be outdone by a kitten, and sang them all a beautiful lullaby that rose to the heavens; enchanting all who heard it. The blackbird really was a beautiful singer. *"Surely this is a great sign of good things to come"* Agnes thought to herself.

It was just as well she could not see into the future, because tomorrow would bring trouble of the kind she could never imagine – and maybe could not escape from!

**

Agnes Is Thrown Away!

Something was happening in the house above them as Archie awoke to a loud scraping, dragging noise that seemed to come from all around him.

"MUM" he shouted out *"what's happening, what is all the noise about?"*

His mother who was already awake, looked across at Archie and gave him a reassuring smile, *"Don't worry Archie, it's just the owners of the house doing a little spring cleaning I imagine"*

BANG! A sudden thump made them both jump up in fright. *"My my, they must be doing some serious cleaning up"* said Agnes *"I'll maybe pop my head out, and see what all the fuss is about."* Agnes climbed up to the little crack in the skirting board and looked out to see what was going on.

Sure enough, the owners had a large selection of old boxes and other stuff, and were taking it out to the car that was sitting with the boot open already half full. In the house a loud electric motor was running as the owner was vacuuming up the mess that they had made.

Agnes knew about these vacuum machines, as she had seen many small creatures being sucked up this long pipe – never to be seen again!

"I'd better make myself scarce before that thing gets anywhere near me." Agnes thought to herself. However just as she was getting ready to disappear back behind the skirting board, she

spotted Archie who had taken another path and appeared on the opposite side of the hallway – right where the vacuum pipe was headed!

"ARCHIE" she shouted over the din of the machine *"ARCHIE...."*

But he could not hear her as he was so engrossed in this wonderful machine – not knowing the danger that it represented. Agnes knew that she had to act fast, if she was to protect her boy from being sucked into the vacuum pipe and never seen again. She ran across the hallway as fast as she could, all the time shouting out Archie's name.

"ARCHIE watch out for goodness sake!" Archie turned around and immediately sensed that his mother was seriously worried.

"Mum, it's all right I'm just watching the machine!" he did not understand the danger he was in.

"Archie get away from here quickly, before it's too late!"

Agnes ran towards him, only to find that the vacuum pipe was now headed in her direction! She tried to scuttle away as fast as she could but too late...she felt the terrible suction as the pipe tried to suck her away up the snout. Quickly spinning a web rope she threw it over an old bent nail in the skirting and held on for her life, as the suction pulled her up the pipe!

She was almost about to let go as her strength left her, when the machine stopped. Immediately she scrambled away, and took refuge in an old cardboard box that was lying in the hallway.

"Phew, that was just too close for comfort there," she thought to herself, as she tried to catch her breath. Another few seconds and I would have been sucked away forever! The very thought of it made her shiver.

Suddenly, her whole world was shaken upside down and she went tumbling around inside the box! It seemed that the box was being lifted off the ground.

"Oh no.." Agnes knew she was in trouble now. She looked out through a little tear in the side and was immediately able to see that she was being carried out to the car. Little Archie was staring wide-eyed at her – but he could do nothing, as the box was put in the back of the car with all the other rubbish.

She was just able to call out before the boot was closed shut.

"Archie, please look after yourself – I'll try to get back to you if I can!" Tears popped into her eyes as the lid was closed and she looked out at her little boy, for what might well be the very last time. Archie was terrified…..he looked over at his mother as the car boot was closed, wondering just what he could do to save her.

"I know, I'll have to call on my good friends, maybe they can help me save mother!" Archie quickly ran back into cover and out through the crack on the outside wall, to call on Suzie and

Jet. *"SUZIE…SUZIE"* he shouted out at the top of his voice – but there was no reply. Suddenly however a dark shape overhead came fluttering down – it was Jet!

"Thank goodness you've come Jet. Mothers has gotten trapped in a big box, and they have put her in the back of that car" Archie blurted out, with large tears forming in his eyes.

"Hold on now Archie, I'm sure it will be all right. I'm happy to help you out, just tell me what you would like me to do." *"Well I would like you to contact Suzie if you can, that way maybe the three of us could help her escape."*

" No problem Archie I'll quickly fly over and see if she is around." Jet flew off to find Suzie. Just a few minutes later Archie could see Suzie bounding across the grass with Jet flying just in front. Archie was in a terrible state when they arrived at his side. *"Archie what has happened?"* Suzie asked as soon as they got near him. Archie quickly explained what had happened to his mum, and how she was trapped in a box that had been loaded into the car. Suddenly an engine started up, and they all turned to see the car disappearing down the driveway of the house!

"Quickly, Jet could you follow the car and see where it is going? If it is not too far away then maybe you could come back and show us where it has gone" *"No worries Archie-boy, I'm right onto it"*

The blackbird flew off in pursuit of the car with Agnes the spider trapped inside it. It seemed to Archie like an age before he came fluttering back again, but in fact it had only been a few minutes. Jet dropped down in front of them to explain.

"We're in luck! They have taken the box to the rubbish skip just down the road, and are even now unloading the boxes amongst the other rubbish. If we hurry down we can find your mum and bring her back again!" Archie and Suzie were ecstatic with this piece of news. *"There is just one thing though"* Jet looked worriedly at them both. *"There are huge seagulls there, that will attack me if I go anywhere near. Do you think you can scare them away Suzie?"*
"Just let me at them, Suzie cried – come on, what are we waiting for?"

Archie quickly jumped up onto Suzie's back and they all headed down the road at full speed for the rubbish tip. In just a few minutes they reached the gate, and sure enough a large flock of hungry seagulls were hovering around eating up anything that they could find. Jet was reluctant to go any further, as they were much bigger than he was and looked very hungry!

Suzie turned to Archie *"Archie, do you want to wait here or do you want to come in with me – you can hide in my furry coat until we get to the boxes where your mum is hiding."*

"That's a great idea Suzie; I'll come with you and help you find her. Jet, you had better keep well hidden until we get back out here"

Jet replied that he would do just that, as Archie and Suzie entered into the tip looking for Agnes. Sure enough the vicious seagulls flocked around them, but Suzie was right, they were very wary as long as she kept her wits about her and lashed out with her sharp claws if they came too near.

Archie meanwhile kept well out of sight as he peeked through her furry coat, and led Suzie to the right pile of boxes. The seagulls circled watching greedily.

"There, over there" Archie spoke into Suzie's ear *"that looks like the right box"* As they got near Archie called out *"MUM….MUM!"* there was no answer. He called out a second time, his voice trembling with fear. *"MUM..MUM..can you hear me? Oh, Suzie I think we may be too late, these horrible seagulls have gobbled her up!"* Archie burst out crying, Suzie did not know what to do. Just then however a tremulous little voice called back

"Is that you Archie?" Agnes looked fearfully from behind an old carton *"Oh it is you!"* Archie jumped off Suzie's back and into his mother's arms, laughing and crying at the same time.

"Hey you two, I hate to break up the party but you have now drawn the attention of these seagulls, it looks like they are about to mob us!

Quickly jump onto my back before they get here, HURRY."

Agnes and Archie jumped onto Suzie's back just in time, as the huge mob of seagulls came swooping down for the attack.

"SCREETCH…We've got you now horrible kitten, you cannot fight us all ha ha!" Suzie bounded towards the gateway out of the tip with this huge mob of screeching seagulls chasing after her, suddenly just a short distance to the gate Suzie was tripped while trying to avoid a peck from a huge orange beak, that would have taken out her eye. Archie and Agnes went flying.

"Ha ha…." The seagulls squawked triumphantly *"we knew you were hiding something from us – nice tasty spiders, just what we love to eat!"* They flew down to gobble up Archie and his mum – it was all over.

Suddenly a black shape shot down amongst the seagulls throwing them into confusion, pecking and making a terrible din. The seagulls didn't know what had hit them at first – but soon realised that it was just a small blackbird, and immediately launched themselves against poor Jet. They pecked and tore at his feathers.

"Run while you can!" Jet called out to them *"hurry, I can't last much longer!"*

Suzie looked at Jet as if to stay *"HURRY NOW!!"* Jet called to them.

Archie and Agnes jumped onto the back of Suzie who immediately took off through the gate, and a little down the road to the safety of a small garden shed, where they could catch their breath. Of Jet there was no sign.

They waited for what seemed like ages, but still there was no sign of their friend.

"I'm going back for him" said Suzie *"wait here and I'll be back in a little while, I promise."*

"Oh do be careful" both Archie and his mum called to her as she left the shed. A few moments later Suzie came reluctantly into their little hideaway.

"I'm so sorry" Suzie said *"there was no sign of Jet anywhere – I think we have lost him to these horrible seagulls!"*

It was a very sad group of friends that made their way back to the house, Archie crying uncontrollably, and Agnes filled with guilt at having been the cause of their misfortunes. Even Suzie, who had had her doubts about their new friend Jet, had to concede that he was a very brave little blackbird to do what he had done. He had saved them all with his bravery – and now he was no more. It was a sad day indeed.

Back at the house, they each looked at one another wondering what to do or say to express their sadness. It was then that they heard a strange crashing sound, from the hedge in front of the garden. They all looked up getting ready to run and hide.

A little black head with a bright yellow beak appeared from the hedge…it was JET!

"Ha ha your alive!" they all rushed over as Jet fell from the hedge.

"Oh no you're hurt!" Archie exclaimed horrified.

"It's nothing serious, I'll be alright in a little while" a bleeding Jet staggered out, to the great concern of his friends.

"But how did you get away from the seagulls?" Suzie was the first to ask the question that they were all wondering.

"Well to be honest I thought it was all over for me, but then a great big lorry came in with a load of rubbish. Not only did they have to let me go as it was headed straight for us, but as soon as it scattered out the old food and rubbish, the seagulls immediately lost interest in me and flew over to get what they could.

I'm sorry it's taken me a little while to get here, but half of my wing feathers have gone, and I can't fly very well at the moment!"

They all excitedly recalled their adventure, and celebrated the safe return of Jet and of course Archie's mum – who immediately insisted that they all have some milk and oatcakes to 'get their strength up'. It had been a hectic day for them all – but a great success for the combined strength of good friends.

There first adventure together had ended well, they had worked as a team to rescue Agnes from the seagulls; and they had proven themselves as friends that would stick together no matter what.

Archie was sure that their adventures together had only just begun.

**

Book 3: Edinburgh Zoo Adventures!

A Trip To The Zoo

Archie had hardly slept a wink all night, the reason being that his mum had told him before he went to bed that she was taking him on a visit to the Zoo the next day, as he had been so good. Now he was up out of his bed and rushing around trying to get all his stuff together; it was still quite cold outside even though it was summer time in Edinburgh. The rain was on again, and Archie's mum said that they would have to be careful of any big pools of water along the way. So with that in mind Archie had looked out his wellington boots, and was not the least afraid of splashing around in the water!

"What about Suzie and Jet" he asked his mum, *"can they come as well? It would be really good to have their company, and I'm sure they would love to see the new spotted bear thingy...Oh a Panda, that's what it's called right?"*
His mother laughed good naturedly, as Archie struggled with the name of the latest additions to

Edinburgh Zoo. It had created a huge fuss in Edinburgh, with people coming from all over just to stare at them through the bars.

"Have no fear Archie; I have already invited them as a wee surprise for you. They should be around shortly in fact. No doubt they are looking forward to seeing the Panda's as well." Said his mum.

Suzie the kitten and Jet the blackbird arrived just a little while later, all excited about going away on their trip to the zoo.

"Hi Archie" they both called out as they arrived at the house *"You'd better get well wrapped up as it is quite cold and windy today"* Said Jet.

"That's ok; I have my jacket and my wellingtons on, so I've no fear of getting cold or wet!"

They all laughed as they looked down at Archie so wrapped up that they could hardly see him. Suzie had a little coat on, but Jet was ok as he did not feel the cold much at all. He was used to perching in a tree all night, no matter how cold it was. Archie's mum Agnes, came out of the kitchen with a shopping bag containing oatcakes and milk, as well as other picnic treats for them all.

Archie had a sudden thought *"but how are we going to get to the zoo mum, it will take us ages if we are going to walk won't it?"*

"Ha ha, you're right Archie. Fortunately for us however, your new friends are going to help us out so we can get to the zoo double-speed!"

Archie looked over happily at Suzie and Jay.

"Yes that's right Archie" said Suzie *"You and your mum can jump on my back, and I'll carry you no problem. We can then hop on board a bus and be there in no time at all. Jet will be able to just fly alongside the bus and meet us when we get off at the zoo, It will work out just fine!"*

As the four intrepid explorers set off for zoo, the weather seemed to improve a little, and they were all hopeful that it would clear enough for a picnic later on in the day. Archie and his mum were safely tucked into Suzie's furry coat, and Jet was flying alongside watching out for the bus. He was ideal for this as he could fly high and see for miles and miles in any direction.

"One day" Archie thought to himself *"I'm going to ask Jet for a ride, and see for myself the entire world – It must be great to be a bird, and not be stuck on the ground all the time like a spider"*

Little did Archie realise, that his wish to fly with Jet would come sooner than he expected – and he would not enjoy the experience at all, in fact, it would maybe put him off flying for life!

They had only been walking for a short while, when Jet called out that there was a bus coming, and it was headed in their direction. They waited patiently at the bus stop, and jumped aboard when the doors opened.

"Normally a bus fare has to be paid when you get on one of these things" Archie's mum explained *"but as we are only small we get on for free!"*

Archie never knew much about money and bus fares and things, but he was happy that his mum did, and that she would look after all that stuff for him.

The bus was quite quiet, and nobody bothered at all when Suzie jumped in and took a seat near the door, where they could all see where they were going. Jet flew alongside the bus for the short journey to Edinburgh Zoo, all the time thinking about the picnic cookies that Agnes had in her bag. *"I should have had a bigger breakfast this morning, I'm starving already and we have just started out!"* He thought to himself while his tummy rumbled.

Before they knew it they were outside the zoo main gates, where Suzie nimbly jumped off and followed the crowd that were obviously going in that direction.

"Oh no" said Archie *"just look at that crowd of people up ahead, please don't tell me they are all going to see the Panda's?"*

"Yes Archie, I'm afraid that exactly what they are doing. It seems that we may never get to see them at all – that queue goes on forever!" Archie's mum said, obviously quite disappointed at the time it was going to take up, just getting to see the Panda's; as there were many more interesting creatures she would have liked to have shown him.

"Listen guys, I know that you would like to get ahead of this queue if you can, so I have an idea" Suzie said to them. Jet on the other hand was not really troubled by this as he could simply fly to the head of the line and watch the Panda's from the nearby tree overhanging the pen. Suzie carried on *"if you just cling tightly to me, then I will be able to climb up that wall and run along the top. That way we can get a view from on high just like Jet – and not get trampled underfoot by the crowds!"*

"What do you think mum?" Archie asked

"Well I think it's a good idea, provided Suzie is confident she will not fall" Agnes said as she looked across at the kitten.

"Fall? Never happen Mrs Brown, I'm as agile as anything on walls and trees, and things – I never fall!"

Encouraged by this bold display of confidence by Suzie, they both clung on tightly as Suzie quickly scrambled onto a low tree and from there onto the wall. Running along the top of the wall and jumping to the occasional tree, they managed to by-bass the ticket office where the big people pay to get in; and were quickly at the Panda enclosure. Suzie was right, they had a fantastic view all over the Panda enclosure from their vantage point; and nobody seemed to mind at all that they had jumped the queue.

"Look mum, there's the Panda's!" Archie excitedly exclaimed. Sure enough the Pandas were sitting out in the sunshine, now that the rain had stopped; and were having a meal of bamboo, which did not look at all appetizing to the onlookers. They were all very high up in a tree at this point and had a great view – apart from a little branch that just seemed to be in the way, no matter how they tried to look around it.

"Hold tight just a minute" said Suzie, *"if I just lean out a bit further......"* SNAP! The thin twig Suzie was leaning on snapped under her, plunging her over the edge of the main branch. Falling over

the edge she just managed to hold on with one sharp claw, almost falling down into the Panda enclosure!

"AARRGGGG….." Archie cried out, as he and his mum tumbled through the air after losing their grip on Suzie's coat. It was a long drop to the ground and they would almost certainly have perished, had not Archie's mum quickly spun a web parachute for them both to cling on to. Slowly they descended to the floor of the enclosure – under the watchful eyes of the Panda's.

"It's all right Archie, I'm sure that they will be friendly Panda's." In fact she was not sure of this at all, but only said that, so that Archie would not be afraid. The Panda's (Tian Tian and Yang Guang, they were called) slowly lumbered towards them, as Agnes desperately looked for some shelter they could hide in – there was nothing!

"Hey you guys!" A familiar voice called out ***"do you need some help there?"*** It was Jet!

"Looks to me like you have gotten yourselves into a bit of bother – am I right?" Jet dropped down beside them. The Pandas were now just a short distance away, and would be upon them soon.

"Jet please stop fooling around, these Panda's may not be friendly and we'd rather not be here

when they reach us – do you have any ideas?"
Archie's mum looked at Jet desperately.
"Well it looks like I will have to save you again! Since that clumsy kitten can't get down here to help you at all" Jet was enjoying being the centre of attention. Agnes glared at him with her strongest stare
"ok, ok here's the plan. Quickly get a tight grip of my feet, and I should be able to fly you up and over that high fence" The both did as they were told, and with a mighty effort Jet lifted off the ground and over the fence, letting them down a short distance away in some nice parkland.

Suzie came running up, looking all shame-faced and awkward.
"It's all right Suzie," Archie's mum said *"thanks to Jet we are all fine now, so don't you be anxious – accidents happen. The main thing is that we are all safe; in fact why don't we just stop here and have some oatcakes and milk before we explore the rest of the zoo?"*
They all nodded their heads vigorously, Jet reminded of just how hungry he was, and Suzie very happy to put the whole incident behind her. Munching away on his biscuits Archie quipped
"The Panda's really were quite beautiful, but I don't think I would like to get so close next time!

And as for that flight to safety – I really thought I was going to fall and be dashed to pieces!" He thought a bit further then asked *"mum, do you think these Panda's would have harmed us at all?"*

"To be honest Archie, I really do not know – however you must remember that although they look cute and cuddly; they are bears!"

They all laughed nervously as they thought of their narrow escape. Edinburgh Zoo is a big place and there were many more strange and exotic animals for them to see before it was time to go home.

**

March Of The Penguins

As the rain had finally stopped, Archie packed away his wet weather gear, and they all cleared up the remains of their picnic, being sure not to leave any rubbish behind on the grass. Everybody was looking forward to the next part of the trip around Edinburgh zoo, and meeting some more strange and exotic animals.

High overhead a great orange beak pointed down at them from the sky, as greedy eyes zoomed in to where the friends were just getting ready to leave. *"Well well, I don't believe it"* Greedyguts (for that was his name) the seagull said to himself *"that looks just like the bunch that escaped me at the rubbish dump!"*

He was referring to the time when Archie had gone to rescue his mum from the dump, and in turn had needed rescued from the attacking hungry seagulls. Jet had managed to save the day, but only by risking his own life in the process.

"Yes it's definitely them – I'll be sure they do not escape this time!" The seagull kept at a distance and awaited his chance to pounce on the unsuspecting friends, happily chatting below.

A sudden commotion opposite from where they were sitting led them all to look across – at a most extraordinary sight! There seemed to be some sort of parade going on, except it was made up of strange looking creatures that Archie had never seen before. They were about 18 inches high, and stood upright on big webbed feet that had claws on the end. What really confused Archie though was that they had very small wings, that did not seem to have any feathers on! Black and white in color with a big yellow/orange patch under their chins, and what seemed like huge beaks to Archie; they were all marching (or waddling really!) in a bunch, much to the delight of the crowds who were making a big fuss and taking lots of pictures.

"Mum, what are these odd-looking creatures" Archie asked.

"why, these are penguins Archie" his mum replied.

"but what ARE they – they look like land creatures, and yet they have wings, or at least something that looks like wings as they do not have any feathers on like Jet here" he motioned over to Jet the blackbird, who was at that moment happily preening himself and sorting out his feathers.

"Ha ha no Archie, they do not fly through the air – they fly through the water instead!"

"the water! How can anything fly through the water – surely that's not even possible" Archie shuddered at the thought of going into deep water, especially as he could not even swim yet. *"Soon I really must go for swimming lessons."* he thought to himself. Archie's mum broke through his thoughts.

"Let's go over there, and I will show you just how easily penguins can fly through the water. They have a large glass swimming pool where you can actually climb under and look onto the penguins swimming around."

They all headed off across to the penguin pool where they hoped to get a wonderful view of the penguins 'flying' in the pool. Everyone laughed as Jet gave his best penguin impression, holding his head up and waddling from side to side as he walked along. Soon they reached the side of the penguin pool, and were lucky enough to get a clear spot as a gap had appeared miraculously in the crowds as they moved along.

"hey hey" cried Archie *"look at them fly through the water!"* *"See I told you so "* his mum said *"although they are actually swimming, they are so fast it looks like they are flying through the air. These little wings cut through the water*

beautifully and push them along at a super speed."

Suzie and Jet were both very impressed, though Jet seemed a bit more grudging than Suzie. *"Well maybe I can't swim like these penguins – but I could surely beat them with my flying abilities! Imagine being a bird that cannot fly – it's just not natural!"* He exclaimed, much to the delight of his companions who thought it was very funny. Soon though the crowds increased again, and they were being pushed along past the glass wall of the pool. *"That was just great"* exclaimed Archie *"where do we go next mum?"*

"Well Archie, I thought we could go along to see the Edinburgh clan of Meerkats – they're called the McMeerkats of Edinburgh zoo! You do have to be VERY careful this time though, because Meerkats are very partial to spiders and they will have you for a tasty little snack if they get any chance at all." They all headed out towards the Meerkats enclosure with Archie holding his mums hand, very excited at meeting this new creature. Overhead meanwhile, Greedyguts the seagull watched their progress. He thought he had lost them amongst all the crowds of people, but he was very patient and now his patience was rewarded when the small group appeared again. He smacked

his beak in anticipation of a tasty meal of fat spider.

As the group were headed toward the Meerkat enclosure, Archie suddenly let out a yelp *"Arrggg, I've lost my bag – I must have left it over at the picnic area."* Sure enough, they all looked across and saw it lying on the grassy spot they had left a few minutes ago.

"I'll get it for you Archie." Said Suzie

"No problem Suzie, I'll manage it myself – it's only a little distance away." Before anyone could say anything else, he pulled his hand away from his mum and ran off to get his bag. They were all completely unaware of a large white seagull greedily watching their every move.

Suddenly Archie's mum looked up and saw the seagull swooping towards him, the others spotted it at just the same time. Archie however, was too concentrated on getting his bag to notice the danger he was in.

"ARCHIE, ARCHIE….." they all cried out to warn him.

"I've got him now!" Greedyguts whooped triumphantly, as he rushed down on Archie. Too late, Archie saw the dark shadow form all around him as the hungry seagull pecked down and captured Archie by the leg. Greedyguts picked him

up and flew off as fast as he could, to a place where he could enjoy a tasty snack of fat spider.

"Woo hoo I'm looking forward to this little snack." Thought Greedyguts, as he settled down on a garage roof a short distance away.

Meanwhile Suzie and Jet took off in the direction of the garage roof, Jet the blackbird reaching it in only a few moments, with Suzie close behind. The seagull dropped Archie for a moment just to gloat over him, before he gobbled him up.

"Well well, not so clever are we now little spider eh!"

"Ouch Mr seagull, you've hurt my leg!" Archie whimpered *"Well now, that won't matter in just a moment – because you are going to make a juicy snack for a hungry seagull. He he – goodbye spider!"* Greedyguts opened his beak wide to swallow up a cowering Archie.

"PECK PECK PECK…." Greedyguts staggered back as Jet pecked the back of his head furiously. *"It's you again,"* cried out the seagull *"well I'm going to fix you good and proper this time."* He left Archie and launched himself against Jet, who was much smaller than the huge seagull. Jet fought bravely, but the seagull was just too big and strong for him, and Jet was soon struggling for his life. Meanwhile though, Suzie the kitten had reached

the garage and leaped up the wall onto the roof. Seeing the danger that her friends were in, she immediately threw herself at the seagull; landing full on its back and scattering it across the roof!

"Get away from my friends" Suzie called out as she opened her sharp claws and beat away Greedyguts the seagull. Greedyguts staggered onto his feet and immediately flapped his large wings to lift himself into the air.

"You've got me this time you horrible kitten – but I'll be watching out for the next opportunity to get my snack!" With that, Greedyguts took off and soared away into the distance, leaving a few crumpled feathers lying around where he had been.

"Are you all right?" A concerned Suzie asked them both. Jet looked a bit pale, but said that he was *"fine"* although he did grumble, *"What took you so long? That seagull almost had us beat!"*

Ignoring Jet, Suzie turned to Archie who was rubbing his leg *"How are you Archie, are you hurt at all?"*

"Just a little bit of a sore leg, but I'll be alright; we'd better get back to mum before she gets too worried."

They all headed back to find a relieved Agnes keeping well hidden, till the coast was clear.

"Archie!" His mum scolded *"don't you ever let go my hand like that again when we are outdoors, do you see how dangerous it can be in the outside world?"* Archie glumly nodded without saying anything. *"Now let me see that sore leg and put a plaster on it for you"* His mum had gotten a big fright and was only cross because she was upset. *"I'm sorry mum, I won't do it again I promise; I just got too excited with things."* Agnes relented as she seen Archie was quite sore and a little upset. *"It's ok Archie, let's get this fixed and go to see the Meerkats – but keep a lookout for that horrible seagull!"* They all nodded that they would do just that, and headed down to the Meerkat enclosure.

"Meerkats are funny things," Archie decided *"always digging and running around looking for food."* He particularly liked the way that they sat up straight, always looking around them and paying attention to everything that was happening. *"I could learn a lesson from them."* He thought to himself as he remembered his close call with the seagull.

As he was looking on, one of the Meerkats suddenly stopped and looked straight at Archie with hungry eyes. *"That's just great,"* he thought to himself *"something else wants me for lunch,*

I'll really have to pay a bit more attention to what's happening around me in future I think."
He did however love the Meerkats, and they all promised to come back again when they had a bit more time.

Meanwhile the day was wearing on and they still had lots of creatures to see before they set off home again.

**

All Creatures Great & Small

"So where do we go next mum?" Archie asked all excited, as they headed further into the zoo.

"Yes Mrs Brown, do we get to see the animals they call Sea lions? I've heard of them but just can't imagine what a lion that lives in the sea looks like!" Suzie said.

"Ha ha you really are funny sometimes Suzie! A Sea lion is not an actual lion at all, but a very large Seal. I think it is called a Sea Lion because the male seal has a very large lion-like head with lots of teeth! The bad news is that I think they may have moved away now, and their enclosure has been filled with little Northern Rockhopper penguins. They are really funny little things with bright red eyes and a yellow crest on their heads." Agnes was a great reader, and followed all the news on what was happening around their little world. The master of the house had a really good book collection, and newspapers were always lying around for her to look at.

"You really know lots Mrs Brown, Archie is very lucky to have a mum like you!"

"That's very kind of you Suzie, but what about your own mother – does she not teach you these things at all?"

Suzie had to explain to her that she was taken away from her mother one morning, when strangers turned up at her master's house and picked her up from her sleeping basket. She had never seen her mother again.

"My new masters are very kind to me though, and I stay in a lovely house where they have made a nice bed for me to sleep in; and I get to go outside whenever I like by using a special little flap they have put into their own door. They are very kind to me really."

"I'm very happy for you Suzie, your new masters sound great. At least as a fluffy kitten you can be quite popular with people; Spiders though are not so popular, as people tend to be scared of us for some reason!"

The little group of friends had been walking along just admiring the exotic creatures all around them, when suddenly Archie exclaimed

"Look at that!"

The all looked in the direction Archie was pointing in, and saw a large head at the end of an extraordinary long neck, reach up into a tall tree;

and with a huge long tongue, pull down a bunch of leaves into its mouth.

"Look at the size of that horse's neck!" Archie cried *"it must have the longest neck in the whole world"*

Jet the blackbird laughed out loud at this *"Ha ha ha ….Archie you really are a hoot – that's not a horse, it's a Giraffe! The all have long necks like that so that they can reach their food, which are the leaves on the topmost branches of trees. I know this because I was sitting on a branch one day minding my own business, when suddenly a large tongue wrapped itself around my leg and almost pulled me into a Giraffes mouth!"*

"Arrggg" Archie exclaimed *"so did you get away alright?"*

"Well luckily for me, Giraffes do not eat birds so he just flicked his tongue, and I was free – but covered in slimy saliva! My feathers were all sticky for ages afterwards"

"Yuuuck!" Archie exclaimed.

They all laughed together at jet's description of his encounter with the Giraffe, which pleased him immensely as he did like to be the centre of attention.

The next visit they had was to the Budongo Chimp enclosure. They were all hugely impressed not only with the Chimpanzees, but the play park that the keepers had built for them.

"Look at these monkeys" Archie shouted excitedly *"I've got to get a bit closer!"* then he struggled to let go of his mums hand so that he could get closer to the fence and reach out to the Chimps inside.

"ARCHIE STOP…" His mother said firmly *"These Chimps may look happy and harmless, but just like any other wild creature they have to be treated with respect, otherwise you could come to great harm. You must always stay behind the barriers – they are there for good reason!"*

Archie stopped his struggling as his mother went on *"Although they look quite innocent, these creatures have the strength of several full grown men – you do not want them to get their hands on you – do you?"*

"No, no definitely not mum – sorry for struggling!"

"That's ok Archie, just remember what happened earlier will you?"

Archie of course remembered the earlier encounter with Greedyguts the seagull, and looked upwards alarmingly at the memory of his narrow escape.

They all continued on their wandering through the Zoo, always pointing and wondering at the many different creatures that they saw. The Elephants especially caused great excitement amongst them, as they marvelled at the size of them and the strangeness of their long noses.

"What else do you know that can pick up a tree by its nose!" Agnes exclaimed happily when an Elephant lifted up a large log by its trunk.

Walking down from the 'African grasslands' part of the park; Jet suddenly flew ahead of them, landing on a tree branch.

"Jet, where are you going." Called Archie.

Archie and his mum had taken a ride on Suzie's back, as they only had little legs and were getting quite worn out with all the walking.

"No-where" Jet called down to them *"just looking that's all"*

"What's he up to I wonder," Suzie said *"he has a mischievous look in his eye I'm sure of it."*

They were walking across a flat area of ground that had strange little holes in it. *"what do you think these holes are for mum?"* Archie asked.

"I really am no….." Archie's mum never finished her sentence when suddenly *"Whooosh"* they were all lifted right off the ground by a massive jet of water.

"Eeeeeekkkkkkkk…." Suzie called out as they all flew up in the air and landed in a pool of water.

"Whooosh…." Another blast of water launched them up in the air again.

Archie and his mum held on for their lives as Suzie bolted for safety. Cats hated water, and now Suzie was frightened and soaking wet!

"Help help.." Suzie called out as she made for the safety of dry ground.

They had walked onto a water spout park, without realizing it. The water was quite harmless really, but it gave you a big fright if you were not expecting it.

As soon as Suzie reached dry ground she gave a big shake, sending Archie and his mum flying through the air.

Fortunately they landed without hurting themselves, in a big web that Archie's mum had spun for them to land on.

Suzie the kitten jumped and pranced around on her tiptoes trying to shake of the water.

"He he ha ha…." Came the sound of laughter from high up in the tree. *"That was truly funny funny funny!"* Jet rocked about holding his sides – almost falling off his perch in fact.

Archie and Agnes just looked at one another and then they too burst out laughing, rolling around on the ground with laughter.

"Oh, that's just fine. Why don't you have a good laugh at my expense," Suzie called out quite indignantly *"look at the mess of my coat! It will take ages to dry – and by the way 'Spider and son' you are going to get wet bottoms when you get back on-board ha ha!"* She stamped her little feet in frustration.

"Come on now Suzie, you are not hurt – and you have to admit it was quite funny!" Archie's mum said as she burst out laughing again.

Suzie eventually seen the funny side of things, and Jet came down from his perch and apologised for leading them into a trap – sort off! He explained that he had been there before and had gotten soaked as well.

"Why don't we all go and sit in the sun to dry off, and we can finish what is left of out picnic before we go home?" Archie's mum said, much to the delight of Jet who was always ready for a piece of Agnes's nice oatcakes.

They spent the rest of the afternoon basking in the sunshine, drying off and eating their picnic. All the while they kept a close watch on the sky for Greedyguts the seagull, just in case he should appear again; fortunately he was nowhere to be seen – although that did not mean he was not out there somewhere!

By this time little Archie was very tired, so they all agreed it was time to head for home. They had all dried out in the sunshine, which Suzie in particular was pleased with; so they started on their way down to get the bus home again.

Archie's mum was very thankful that the trip home went without any more drama – she had had quite enough for one day.

"Thanks very much Suzie and Jet, for accompanying us on our trip today." she said to Archie's new friends *"I'm very happy that you came – and for rescuing Archie from that horrible seagull!"*

Jet and Suzie both agreed that they had had a great time at the zoo, and they all made a promise to return again sometime soon; as there was a lot to see and just not enough time for people with little legs to see it in one day.

They all returned to their homes for a sleep, Archie in particular wondering what the next day would bring – and what news friends he might meet!.

**

Book 4: Heroic Rescues & Sea Monsters!

The Good Samaritan

The sun was shining as Archie set of for his snack down by the riverside. It was in fact a little stream that flowed over a drop, to create a bright shining waterfall leading in to a beautiful clear pool of water. Archie loved to sit here and watch the fish as they played around in the shallow water, often basking in the warmth of the sunshine as it bounced and flickered over the surface.

His mum had made up a little hamper for Archie, and told him to be very careful down by the water, as it could be quite dangerous if you fall in!

"But I'm not afraid of falling in mum; I can just spin a little spider's web raft and float on the surface!" Archie said smugly

"Oh yes Archie," said his mother with a smile on her face *"but what happens when a big greedy fish fancies a little spider for his lunch? You would be gobbled up before you know it!"*

Archie shuddered as he thought of being swallowed down into the depths of a big fish's mouth

"You're right mum, but don't worry I will be very careful not to go too near the water's edge."

He had just reached the stream and was walking along whistling a little tune to himself, when he was suddenly aware of a little squeaky voice calling out for help.

"Help me somebody, please!" A little voice said from just up ahead on the opposite side of the water

"I wonder what that could possibly be."

Archie thought to himself, as he got nearer the sound of the little voice

"It sounds like someone is in trouble!"

Soon he was near enough to see that the sad little voice was coming from a little mouse, that was obviously injured and laying down in the wet grass looking totally miserable. *"Hey can I help you at all?"* Archie called out across the water

"Oh please!" The little mouse responded

"I've been lying here for ages, and nobody has helped me at all; in fact they have just passed by and left me here bleeding!"

"Ok, I will try and help you, but first I have to try and get across the water. There is a bridge a little

way upstream, just hold on and I will cross over to you and see what I can do to help."

"Oh please hurry, I'm feeling very faint after lying here for ages, and I really don........"

The little mouse's voice trailed off as he fell into a faint.

"Oh no!" Archie thought to himself

"I can't waste time getting to the bridge, I'll have to try and get across here!"

Looking up at the trees overhead Archie quickly devised a plan

"If I can just lasso a web rope over that high branch, then I could swing across to the other side easily - surely!"

He quickly spun a rope and swinging it around his head, he threw it with all his might – and missed the branch!

However Archie was a very determined and stubborn little spider, so he continued throwing the lasso until finally on the fourth throw…

"YES I've got it!" He was jubilant, and got the rope wrapped around his body as he prepared to launch himself over the stream; it was then that he looked down into the water – and seen the greedy fish looking up at him from the depths!

"Oh no – mum was right. If I fall in to this water, I will end up as food for the fishes!"

The little mouse over on the other side of the stream gave out a little moan

"Just hold on little mouse, I'm coming over right now."

Decision made; Archie launched himself into the air swinging from the branch of the tree out over the water -where the fish were watching him intently. Suddenly as Archie reached about halfway across, the largest of the fish jumped right out of the water and opening its mouth wide, prepared to gobble up poor Archie!

"Oh no you don't!" Archie called out as he very quickly climbed higher up his web-swing; just as the fish closed its mouth over fresh air!

Archie landed safely on the other side of the stream, and quickly rushed up to the little mouse

"Are you all right little mouse?" He cried out as he approached

"Not really, in fact I do not feel well at all!" The mouse replied

Archie quickly set himself to work and bandaged up the wounds with his special web-bandage.

"What exactly happened to you little mouse?" Archie said

"Please, my name is Tiny."

"Ok then Tiny, my name is Archie; how did you get into this state?"

"It was terrible; I was walking along minding my own business when a group of bullies came along and pushed me around, beat me up and stole the cheese sandwiches that mum had prepared for my lunch."

"But did no-one offer to help you!" Archie said, shocked that such a thing could happen in his neighbourhood.

"No-one helped me at all; in fact you are the first one to offer – everyone else just passed by and said it was none of their business!"

"Well never you mind," said Archie: *"I'm here now and I am going to get you home. Do you live far away?"*

"Well I'm away down at the bottom of the garden, and my leg is very badly hurt – I don't think I can walk at all!"

Tiny looked thoroughly miserable as she looked at Archie, in obvious pain from her injuries.

Archie rubbed his little chin as he wondered how on earth he was going to get this little mouse home, after all even though he was little – he was far too heavy for Archie to carry!

Suddenly Archie's face lit up

"Ha! I know; I'll call on my friend Suzie and she can maybe carry you home!"

"But who is Suzie?" Tiny exclaimed.

"Why, Suzie is my friend the kitten."

Tiny looked at Archie totally horrified

"A KITTEN! – But Archie, a kitten will just eat me up! Don't you know that cats do not like mice at all?"

Archie patiently explained that Suzie was not any old kitten – but that she was Archie's special friend, and she would certainly not eat Tiny if Archie asked her not to.

"Honestly Tiny, you will be all right I promise!"

Tiny looked thoroughly unconvinced as Archie whistled loudly a special whistle that he had developed, so loud that Suzie could hear the sound a long way away.

After what seemed like an age, the white furry shape of Suzie the kitten appeared on the opposite bank of the stream.

Tiny shrank back trying to hide behind Archie as the kitten called out:

"Hi Archie, what's happening – do you need some help at all?" Just then Suzie's eyes landed on Tint the mouse

"It's a mouse!" Suzie exclaimed as she bounced up and down excitedly *"Can I play with her Archie?"*

Archie was very aware that when a cat played with a mouse, it usually ended up badly for the mouse!

"No Suzie, you cannot play with her. This little mouse is called Tiny, and she has been beaten up by some bullies who stole her lunch and left her abandoned here. She cannot walk and I need your help to get her home!"

Suzie looked slightly puzzled at Archie

"But Archie, don't you know that cats and mice don't make good friends – it just is not normal for a cat to help a mouse!"

"Suzie, please listen to me. How would you like it if you were beaten up like Tiny here, and no-one helped you? In fact, didn't I rescue you from that horrible dog – and look what great friends we've become! Just think; one day this little mouse may just be able to help you – you really never know what lies ahead, and it is always good to have friends you can rely on to help you out in times of trouble."

Suzie thought to herself that Archie really was a clever friend to have – she would never have thought of all that!

"Ok, Archie, I do see your point – so I'll help out your little mouse friend."

"Her name is Tiny" Archie said as he made the introductions. Tiny the mouse however did not looked totally convinced, still cowering behind Archie as Suzie bounded across some rocks that

were placed in the stream; reaching Archie and Tiny in just a few moments.

"Ha, I wish you were here earlier – you could have carried me across!" Archie exclaimed

Tiny the mouse spoke up

"I'm not letting that kitten carry me Archie – I'm sure she will just eat me!"

"Suzie, you must promise me before Tiny here – that you will not eat her! Would that make you happy?" Archie asked the timid mouse. Tiny agreed, and so Suzie solemnly promised that she would not eat her, but instead carry her across and see her safely home.

"Ok, so it's agreed," said Archie as he jumped up on to Suzie's back. Tiny however could not climb up onto Suzie as her leg hurt so badly, and Archie could not help either.

"I know," Said the kitten *"do you trust me now Tiny?"*

"I, I th.. think so" Tiny replied through trembling lips

Suzie carefully leaned down and gripped Tiny by the tail very gently.

"Hey hey, that's a great idea Suzie! Now let's head across the river and to Tiny's home – but be careful you do not drop her!"

Tiny the mouse swung around under Suzie's chin as they made their way to her home under the blackberry bushes, at the end of the garden. In just a few minutes they all arrived safe and sound.

"Here you are Tiny!" Archie said as Suzie dropped her gently in the soft grass *"Will you make it inside your home ok do you think?"*

Tiny looked up at Archie, who was still on Suzie's back

"No problem at all, my mum will sort me out ok. You guys are just great, and I can't wait to tell my mum what just happened – she will be so pleased! If I can do anything at all for you, please just call on me – but try not to scare mum!"

Suzie and Archie said their farewells and Suzie bounded off to Archie's home where they told Archie's mum Agnes all about their adventures rescuing Tiny the mouse.

Agnes just shook her head in wonder – who knows just what her brave little guy will be up to next? He was certainly making a big impact on their little community.

**

Archie Dreams a Dream

Archie woke up with a bit of a headache, his nose was running and he did not have a good night's sleep at all. In fact he had been awake for most of the night, so that now he just felt 'all washed out' and really did not feel like getting out of bed at all.

"Archie!" His mother called up to him. *"Are you going to get out of bed anytime soon? If you stay there any longer, it will soon be time for bedtime again!"*

Archie groaned into his blankets and buried his head into the pillow, hoping that his mum would just leave him in bed.

A few moments later, the door flew open and his mum stood there, hands on hips.

"Come on young man, what on earth is wrong with you today?" She threw back the covers, to find poor Archie shivering and covered with sweat!

"Oh, Archie, you're not well. What on earth is the matter with you?" She asked her little boy, who was looking more miserable by the minute.

"I don't know mum, I have had a horrible night. My head aches and my nose is all running. Can I stay in bed a little while longer – I really do not feel like I can manage very well at all."

Archie's mum Agnes, immediately felt bad for trying to get him out of bed, when he obviously was not well with what looked like a bad cold.

"Don't you worry Archie; I think you have a bad cold, so you stay in bed while I mix you up a hot lemon drink. Is your throat sore at all?"

"Well yes now that you mention it, my throat does feel a bit sore!" Archie replied miserably.

"Well that's to be expected Archie, you have a bit of a cold but never mind, I will put some honey in your hot drink and this will soothe your throat also."

Agnes immediately set off to make his hot drink.

"What a shame for Archie," she thought to herself, *"But I'm sure this hot toddy will help him out. I'll have to keep him in bed for the day, maybe more."*

Archie lay back in bed, feeling quite exhausted and very weak. He had planned to go out today with Suzie and Jet for some more adventures around the garden, but he really was not up for it at all.

"They will be disappointed that I can't get out playing." Archie thought. *"But never mind I'm sure I will be fine very soon, mum will sort me out in no time."*

Archie's mum soon came back up to the room with a hot drink for him.

"Here you are Archie, now drink it all up; it will help you to get a little sleep and I'll drop by in a little while to see how you are."

"Thanks mum, I'm sure I'll feel better soon."

Archie said, as he cradled the hot drink carefully, in case he spilled it and burned himself.

Archie took his time and blew on the hot drink until it was cool enough, then he sipped carefully until he had finished the lot. He hadn't realised just how thirsty he was, but now he felt really sleepy and soon fell off into a sound sleep.

Archie was dreaming, and in his dream he seemed to be swinging from a wall somewhere dark and damp. He did not know why, but for some reason it was important that he should get across to the other side. It seemed that he was in a cave of some sorts, and he was being watched by a man who was obviously hurt and very tired looking.

He was getting tired of all the work involved with swinging out to reach the other side of the cave, but he just had to do it, so he battled on, swinging back and forward, each time getting a little nearer the other side. Once or twice he slipped, plummeting down to the bottom of the cave. A little bruised and battered, he still had to climb back up again which took great effort as he was now very tired.

At last on the seventh massive attempt, he swung out into the cave and managed finally to reach the opposite wall – exhausted but exhilarated with his achievement.

In this strange dream, it seemed that the man jumped up and down with excitement at Archie's achievement – even shouting out *"SPIDER, YOU'VE DONE IT!"*

Then the man rushed out of the cave shouting on his men- who were gathered outside to pick up their weapons.

It was all strange to Archie, who in the dream, just carried on making his web – for that was obviously why he had wanted to get to the other side of the cave.

Archie awoke with his mother wiping his head with a wet cloth. It was now late in the day, as he had slept right through to supper time, he was so exhausted.

"Archie, Archie...are you ok?"

Archie looked up into the very concerned looking face of his mother.

"Y..Yes mum, I..I think so" He said just a little confused.

"You're ok Archie," said his mum soothingly, *"you just have a little fever. I heard you talking in your sleep and came up to see what was going*

on. I've just been wiping your forehead with a cool cloth. How do you feel now?"

"Well I think I'm a little better." Archie said. *"But I did have a very strange dream, where I was making a web in a dark cave!"*

Archie's mum explained that strange dreams were quite common when you had a high temperature, and could be very strange indeed because of the fever and the headache.

"Why don't you tell me all about it Archie, if you're well enough that is." Agnes said.

So Archie went into a lengthy explanation of what he had seen in the dream, trying to remember everything and miss out no detail. When he had finished the story he was quite tired out again from the effort. He slumped down into the pillow.

His mum was giving him a strange look, so much so that Archie grew concerned.

"Mum, what is it?"

"Oh Archie, it's nothing to worry about at all.."

Archie's mum hesitated as if deciding whether or not to tell her little boy something.

"Come on mum, I know something's bothering you – have I done something wrong maybe?"

Archie grew increasingly concerned.

Agnes made a decision, and looked down at Archie lying in his bed.

"Well I don't suppose it will do any harm to tell you a little story – since you are in bed anyway!" Agnes said playfully to put Archie at his ease.

"You see Archie, there is a tradition in our family that a very distant relation of ours - your great grandfather many times over - was responsible for encouraging one of the greatest Kings that Scotland ever had; to continue and never give up, no matter what.

It so happened that Fergus - that was his name – was fixing himself a new home up in a highland cave one day, when a warrior came into the cave seeking shelter and a place to rest. Fergus was a bit put off by this intrusion, and so it took him longer than he expected to get the web across to the other side of the cave. In fact it took seven attempts before he managed it.

The warrior meanwhile was watching him intently, and Fergus was concerned that he might mean to harm him. However it was exactly the opposite, and when Fergus managed to finally get across on his seventh attempt the warrior jumped up and congratulated him; saying that he had never seen such determination in something so small."

"Spider, what is your name?" The warrior asked Fergus.

"Why, my name is Fergus."

"Well Fergus I thank you for this lesson, in fact the whole of Scotland thanks you, for I am King Robert the Bruce of Scotland, and your perseverance in the face of adversity will be passed down through the ages, and you will be a legend amongst the folks of my fair land!"

Agnes continued, *"with that said, King Robert left the cave and continued to do battle and defeat the English King – on his seventh battle!*

Ever since then, the Scottish people have remembered the story of King Robert and the Spider who helped him defeat an army!"

"So my great , great, great…….Grandfather was a real hero!"

"Yes Archie, indeed he was – and I'm sure you will be as well one day! Now, time for some sleep and I'm sure you will be fine and well by tomorrow."

Archie was indeed exhausted because of his cold, and he just managed to mumble a *"goodnight mum"* before he drifted off into a deep sleep.

Archie had to get his strength up for the next adventure that lay ahead…

**

Archie Goes To The Beach

Archie was jumping up and down, all excited with the news that his mum had just given him – they were going to the beach for a special treat.

Archie had never been to the beach before, but he had heard lots about it and was really excited to see it for himself. First of all though he had to help his mother get the hamper packed with all kinds of goodies to eat, along with blankets to sit on (The sand gets everywhere, his mum said); and he had to look out his bathing costume if he wanted to go for a paddle.

"Now remember Archie," his mum said wagging her finger at him. *"You are not to get out of your depth in the sea, as it can easily sweep you out of sight, and I might never find you again."*

Of course he promised to be careful, and not get into trouble at all.

"What about your friends Suzie and Jet, do you think they would like to come at all?" Archie's mum Agnes asked.

Archie jumped up and down again, *"oh yes I'm sure they would, can I go and shout for them? It would be so good if they could come along"*

With his mum's approval, Archie sped out to look for his friends. Jet the Blackbird was sitting high on a tree branch, and immediately swooped down when he seen his friend Archie.

"Hi Archie, what's up? You look very excited about something!"

"Oh Jet, mum is going to take us all on a trip to the beach, where we can play in the rock pools and maybe even paddle in the sea. There will be all sorts of fun to be had there I'm sure! Would you like to come with us? – it would be great if you could."

"I'd love to come to the beach with you, what about Suzie?" Jet said. *"Can she come also?"*

"Of course she can! In fact I wondered if you could fly over to her house and ask her for me." Jet replied that it would be no trouble at all, and immediately flew off to speak to Suzie; who at that moment was chasing some dried leaves that were blowing around her garden.

"SUZIE." Jet called out to get her attention.

"Oh, hi Jet. Sorry, I was a bit occupied chasing these leaves – I just think they are very funny and love to chase them around!"

"Hmmm," Jet said *"I really think you are easily pleased sometimes!"*

"Of course I am, I am a kitten after all, and this is what kittens do!" Suzie said quite indignant.

"Ok, never mind Suzie. I'm here because Archie wondered if you would like to join us for a trip to the beach. We will be leaving in a little while, when his mum has finished packing the hamper."
"Oh yes, that would be great – I've never been to the beach before, have you?"
"Well yes in fact I have, but I was only a kid at the time and don't remember much about it really." Jet said.

"Well, it sounds like good fun anyway, though of course I will not be going for a swim – I really do not like water very much. What I am looking forward to is jumping down these sand dunes I've heard about! Let's go before they leave without us."

With that, Suzie bounded away towards Archie's house, while Jet flew along overhead.

They arrived at the house just as Archie and his mum were coming out, and so the merry band of travellers headed off to catch the local bus down to Gullane beach.

The journey took no time at all, as they all chattered together about what they would do when they got there. Archie was particularly keen on finding strange creatures in the rock-pools, that had been left behind with the tide. While Jet wondered what kind of snacks Archie's mum Agnes had packed for them!

"Hey hey," Archie shouted out as they all jumped of the bus and headed over the grassy area to the beach.

"Remember Archie, and stay close to me – I do not want you getting lost amongst the dunes. In fact why don't we both jump up on Suzie's back until we get to our picnic spot – is that ok with you Suzie?" Agnes said.

"Certainly, that would be no trouble at all, just remember to hold on tight!"

They both climbed onto Suzie's back and spun a little web to keep them secure.

"Ok Suzie, we're ready!" Agnes called out.

Suzie immediately bounded away down to the sand dunes bordering the beach front, while Jet flew on ahead feeling just a little bit superior, not being stuck to the ground like everybody else.

The beach was quite busy, with people out walking with their dogs, and lots of birds – including seagulls!

"I hope Greediguts is not amongst them." Archie thought to himself.

Greediguts was a Seagull that had almost eaten Archie, when he had gone on a trip to the zoo.

Only the quick thinking and a rescue by Jet and Suzie had saved him from being all swallowed up! *"Never mind, I will not let a horrible Seagull ruin my day at the beach."* Archie spoke out loud without meaning it.

"What's that you said?" Suzie asked Archie.

"Oh nothing at all, I was just saying that we should be careful of these Seagulls over there." Archie pointed to the distance.

"No worries Archie, I've got my eye on them!" Said Suzie; who then lost her footing and went summersaulting down the last sand-dune before the beach.

"Aarrggggg." They all cried out as she tumbled head over heels, landing in a heap face-down into the soft sand at the bottom!

They all got up unharmed, coughing and spluttering sand out of their throats; to hear Jet the Blackbird roaring and laughing from a perch in a thorn bush.

"Now that was funny, he he he! I bet you wish you could fly like me!"

"Why would I wish such a thing?" Suzie said, *"Then I would not be able to have all this fun!"* Immediately after she let Archie and Agnes jump down from her back, she ran straight back up

again, and launched herself back down the sand-dune.

"Whey hey! This is great fun!" Suzie shouted out. Archie and his mum both laughed at Suzie who was so easy to please. – Jet just shook his head in wonder.

"Ok, Archie," Agnes said *"I think I will just lay out the blankets here in this nice cosy spot. We have a great view of the sea and it is nice and sheltered from the wind. If you want to go and explore with your friends, I will set out our little picnic for you coming back. Remember though, stay close enough to shout out if you need me!"* Jet decided to stay with Agnes for now, and help her with the picnic. Really he was just hoping to get a sneaky biscuit, if he helped out – he was always a little 'peckish' was Jet.

Suzie went bounding off with Archie on her back, his little shoulder bag bouncing up and down; as she headed to the water's edge where there were many rock-pools to explore.

Jumping down from Suzie's back Archie said, *"look Suzie, there are tiny fish swimming around in this pool."*

"You're right Archie." Said Suzie as she gingerly dipped in her paw to try and catch some.

"Brrrrrr, that's freezing!" She cried out, withdrawing her paw quickly from the water.
"Ha ha, well it is Scotland you know. The water's seldom actually warm!" Archie said, just a little smugly to his good friend.

Just at that a bunch of feathers that had been caught up in the wind, went tumbling past Suzie; who immediately took off after them shouting excitedly. The feathers picked up speed as the wind carried them just out of reach, of her claws as she leapt after them.

"SUZIE!" Archie called after her, but it was no good. She was totally caught up in her game.

"Ah well, never mind," thought Archie, *"I'll just explore these pools till she comes back again."*

Archie hadn't noticed that a tiny pair of beady eyes had been watching him all this time, and a huge pair of claws snapped open and shut anticipating a nice spider meal!

Archie moved past the first pool that had all the little fish, and explored some of the others. He seen little crabs and shellfish stuck to rocks, and lots of other creatures that he had absolutely no idea what they were; in fact most of the underwater creatures were a complete mystery to him!

He wandered back to the first pool again, and peered down into the crystal clear water.

"What on earth is that thing moving amongst the weed?" Archie though, as he detected some movement.

All the while the claws clicked in anticipation.

"I just cannot make it out at all." Archie thought to himself, as he put his head closer to the water's surface.

The giant red Crab moved a little closer.

"SNAP SNAP SNAP!" Went the crabs huge claws as it lunged up at Archie from the depths.

"Aarrgggggg." Archie called out as he leapt back – but just not quite fast enough, as one of the huge claws caught a hold of his shoulder bag.

The Crab got a tight grip and gradually started to pull Archie down to the water's edge.

"HELP… HELP!" Archie called out, but nobody could hear him as he was just a little too far away, and his voice was lost in the breeze that had picked up.

Archie struggled to get the shoulder bag off, but with the Crab pulling, it was just impossible.

Now his feet were in the cold water and he was being pulled ever deeper, as the Crab tugged and pulled, as it eagerly anticipated a tasty meal of plump Spider!

"HELP…HELP!" Archie called out again, really scared now as he could not get away from the Crab, and the freezing water was now up to his waist!

"I can't get away, and nobody can hear me shout. But there is no way I'm going to let this giant sea monster eat me!"

With that thought, and just as he was up to his neck in water, Archie give a final giant heave. He was in luck! The strap holding the bag around his shoulder gave a mighty snap, and he was free. Leaping out of the pool before the 'monster' could get another hold of him.

"Phew, that was a very close call." He thought to himself. *"Now I'm soaking wet and freezing as well!"*

"Hi Archie, what's happening – have you been for a swim?" Suzie said cheerfully as she reached Archie's side.

"A SWIM! I was almost eaten by a giant sea monster, while you were off chasing a bunch of dried feathers down the beach!" Archie cried out indignantly.

He explained what had happened to Suzie, who despite herself could not help but give a little snigger.

"You're laughing? This is not funny, I just escaped being a monsters lunch – no thanks to you!"

"Seriously Archie," said Suzie, *"there are no monsters in seaside pools. Let me have a look and see for myself.*

"STOP, please be careful." Archie said fearfully. *"It might even drag you in as well!"*

Just to humour Archie, Suzie carefully went over and peered down into the water.

Looking up at her was the small beady eyes of a huge Crab, with its large claws raised ready to snap at her!

"Aarrggg, you're right Archie. Look at the size of that!"

Just then Jet appeared.

"What's all the fuss about here then? And why are you all wet Archie?"

Suzie spoke first.

"Archie got attacked by a giant sea monster, and almost get himself eaten!"

"Whaaat! You must be imagining things again Suzie – there is no such things as monsters!" Jet laughed to himself.

"Oh yes there is!" Archie said. *"Just look over there into that pond and see for yourself!"*

"All right I'll do it just to keep you happy – but there are no sea monsters!"
Jet hopped over to the side of the pool and looked in.

The giant Crab lunged out of the depths and caught hold of Jet by one feather!

"Arrgggg, help." Cried Jet, as they all grabbed hold of him and managed to pull him away from the 'monster' minus his feather!

"Now do you believe us?" Both Suzie and Archie called out triumphantly.

"Well that was unbelievable!" Jet admitted.

"Let's get back to your mum Archie – I'll bet she has an explanation, as I'm almost positive there are no such things as sea monsters – certainly not on Gullane beach!"

They all headed back, chattering excitedly about the 'sea monster' that had almost eaten them up.

"Ha ha ha.." Agnes laughed good naturedly at them. *"A sea monster indeed! By your description I would say that you have just encountered a giant Crab that's all – but big enough to have you for lunch by the sound of it Archie! Now why don't you all sit down in the sunshine, and we can have our picnic while you dry out."*

"Yes, that's a great idea." Said Jet; who had not managed to sneak any food at all while Agnes was unpacking.

So they all sat down and got tucked into fresh oatcakes, and cheese & pickle sandwiches which they all loved. Agnes had even packed some tuna fish sandwiches which Suzie thought were the most fantastic thing she had ever eaten!
"Arrggg. Now I know why they are called SANDwiches!" Moaned Archie as he spat out grains of sand from his mouth.
"Here Archie," said his mum, *"try a wee drink of this Irn Brew to wash the sand away!"*
They all had a good laugh as they eat up their food, anticipating a great day ahead on the beach; unaware of the large white Herring-gull that was circling high overhead…
……**To Be continued in Book 5**

Bonus Story
Archie's Crispy Cakes

Archie was bored. It was pouring rain outside and he was pacing up and down, desperate to get out and play with his friends Suzie and Jet. The weather – and his mum – however had other ideas. *"It's no use you pacing up and down Archie,"* his mum said *"this rain is not going to stop any time soon, so you might as well do something constructive; instead of moping around the house!"*

Archie looked across at his mother Agnes. *"But what can I do, I'm bored silly, and there is nothing to do around here!"* Archie replied feeling a bit depressed by it all.

"Nothing to do indeed!" Said Agnes. *"What about cleaning up your bedroom, and putting all your dirty washing in the basket where it belongs. Your room is an absolute tip, in fact I found an old toffee stuck to your bed sheets yesterday and if that had got stuck in your hair you would have been in a right mess!"*

"Oh mum," Archie replied a bit sheepishly. *"You know that's not what I meant. I will tidy up my*

room honest, but isn't there something a bit more exciting to do – I mean, tidying my room is just not any fun at all."

Agnes looked over at her little boy and put on her sternest face. *"Well Archie, it's about time that you learned something about this life – it is not all about having fun! However,"* She said with a much softer voice, as she could not be annoyed with Archie for long. *"Maybe you would like to help me in the kitchen? – We could maybe make some chocolate crispy cakes!"*

"Yea….that's more like it!" Said Archie jumping up and down with excitement. *"Can we add raisins as well?"* Said Archie.

"Yes of course you can, now go and get washed up and we can get started melting the chocolate."

"Oh, and what about some mini-marshmallows?"

"Yes, yes. Now go and wash your hands!"

Archie rushed off to wash his hands, which seemed a little strange to him, as they would soon be covered in chocolate, which would have to be washed off again! *"Adults can be very strange sometimes,"* thought Archie. *"but never mind, I will just lick the chocolate from my fingers when mum's not looking, he he."*

It took Archie a few minutes to wash his hands – which in fact could also be feet – meaning that he had 8 feet (or hands!) to wash. However as soon as he was ready he jumped up into a high chair by the kitchen worktop, balancing four feet on the chair and leaving four 'hands' to help his mum.

"Right mum, what do you want me to do now?" Archie asked.

"Just you sit right there," Agnes replied. *"and I will bring you over the rice-crispies. I have already added the chocolate into a bowl over some hot water, and in a few minutes it will be melted enough for you to mix the chocolate through. Then you can add the raisins and the mini-marshmallows."*

A few minutes later and the chocolate was thoroughly melted.

"Ok Archie, I'm going to place the bowl of melted chocolate next to you, and you must carefully pour in the rice crispies, as well as the raisins and the marshmallows – can you manage that ok?"

"Of course I can manage that, I'm not a baby you know!" Archie said indignantly. He quickly reached over for the packet of rice crispies – and promptly sent the marshmallows flying off the table and rolling all over the kitchen floor!

"ARCHIE! I told you to be careful – now look what you've done!"

"I'm sorry mum; I don't know how that happened at all!" Archie said a little downcast. *"Ok, we will leave it for now – but you will help me clean them all up after we have finished. You're lucky I have some spare mini-marshmallows in the cupboard; now let's try again – slowly this time!"*

So very carefully Archie added the rice crispies to the melted chocolate, along with the marshmallows and a handful of raisins. Then with a wooden spoon in each of his four hands, he set to work mixing it altogether.

"Yummy!" Said Archie desperate to lick the end of a spoon – at least one! "What do we do now mum?"

Agnes arranged some paper cup-cake containers on the table in front of Archie. *"That's a good job little man!"* She said smiling. *"Now all you have to do is add some of the mixture to each of the little holders – careful now, you do not want to waste any!"*

Archie carefully dipped in a spoon and filled the containers one by one. He was tempted to try and fill two at a time, as he was using four hands, but decided not to risk it – not after scattering the marshmallows all over the floor!

Agnes set to work cleaning up the mess as Archie set to his task; she had relented and decided to let Archie off with cleaning up the wasted marshmallows.

"Never mind," Agnes thought to herself, *"he is just a little keen to get the job done – and no doubt to lick all four spoons clean of chocolate!"* She could have in fact been reading Archie's mind – mums are good at that!

"He he, there's loads of chocolate stuck to these spoons, and there's no way I'm going to drop them in a sink full of soapy water before I have licked them all clean!" Archie mischievously glanced over his shoulder, sure that his mum suspected nothing!

Agnes dutifully pretended not to notice as Archie finished filling up the paper cups – and promptly licked clean all four spoons in record time!

"Right mum, that's me finished." Archie called over.

"Just look at that," said Agnes *"and have you washed up the spoons already – they look very clean to me!"*

"Em, ah well, I thought I would just lick of the sticky chocolate in case it blocked up the sink, em.. maybe?"

Agnes laughed out loud.

"Ha ha ha well that's the best excuse I've heard for a while Archie – it's ok though I'm sure there was not a lot left on the spoons anyway."

"No that's right mum, there was not much left at all."

Even as Archie said this, he was feeling just a little queasy; in fact he was feeling decidedly sick and the mere mention of chocolate caused him to put his hand to his mouth.

"What is it Archie? You look decidedly unwell – do you think you have had too much sticky, sweet gloopy chocolate?" Agnes teased him.

It was all too much for poor Archie and he jumped down off the stool and raced for the bathroom – where he promptly puked up a sticky mess of chocolate, raisins and marshmallows!

Agnes followed him through, just to make sure that he was ok. Lessons have to be learned sometimes, and one of the earliest lessons is not to eat too much chocolate – or you will be sick!

Archie came out of the toilet in a few minutes, still a little unsteady on his feet. *"Oh mum, I really do not feel well."* Said Archie, with a moan.

"Well I am hardly surprised young man. I saw you sneaking the chocolate from the spoons, and you have simply eaten far too much. You had

better go and lie in your bed for a wee while, and you will be as right as rain before you know it."

"But what about the crispy cakes mum, I should give you a hand put them away?" Archie managed a pathetic little groan that said he would much rather get to his bed though.

"Never mind that Archie, I will put them aside for you and your friends and you can invite them all round in the morning for tea and cakes – I'm sure Jet in particular is partial to a chocolate crispy cake!" Agnes laughed, as Jet the blackbird was always hungry it seemed.

"Oh that's a great idea mum! Actually I feel better already, maybe I shou….." Archie quickly clamped his hand to his mouth and raced back into the bathroom to be sick again!

"No you don't Archie, you will have to lie down for a while until your poor stomach settles down from your overeating!"

After a few minutes Archie re-appeared looking decidedly unwell.

"You're right mum, I'll just lie down for a wee while and I'm sure I'll be fine."

"Oh poor Archie!" Agnes said as she lifted him into her strong arms, and carried him off to bed where he could have a little sleep and feel a lot better after it.

In no time at all Archie was drifting off to sleep dreaming of his picnic in the morning with his good friends Suzie and Jet.

"I do hope Jet does not eat all the cakes!" Was Archie's last thought, as sleep overtook him.

**

More

Thanks for reading my stories on the adventures of Archie the Friendly Spider; I hope you have enjoyed reading them as much as I have enjoyed writing them!

The adventures of Archie will continue as more books follow this one, and Archie and his friends find themselves in more 'situations' that have to be dealt with.

Shameless plug!

Please recommend this book to your friends if you have enjoyed it – a review on Amazon would be very much appreciated.

Till the next adventure....

J W Paris

Resources

A particular thanks for the great artwork goes to my good friend Agnieszka Gorak. You can see more examples of her unique sense of humor and observations on life, at her website www.myguineapigtales.co.uk

27241050R00063

Printed in Great Britain
by Amazon